Dedicated to
my very own
cuddle monster,
Sirius.

The Bibalibet

THE LOST SMILE

Have you ever met the Bibalibet?

You would know it if you had. He is friendly, soft and cuddly and he really loves to laugh.

He loves climbing trees and staring at the sky.

He loves waving excitedly at all the animals as they pass him by.

But one day, the Bibalibet woke up and he felt strange.

He tried to laugh
but he couldn't.
He tried to smile
but he couldn't.

The Bibalibet decided to ask his friends to help him find his smile.

He went to the edge of the forest, where he found his friends the hyenas.

"Will you help me find my smile?" he asked them with a frown.

They were laughing and joking about who could burp the loudest.

This annoyed the Bibalibet, because their burps were so loud that they couldn't even hear him.

So the Bibalibet went to see his friends the chimpanzees and asked, "Will you help me find my smile?" but they were so busy chasing each other and laughing wildly that they didn't even notice him.

The Bibalibet felt sad because he couldn't catch up to them and he still couldn't find his smile.

Finally he went to see his friends, the toddlers in the park.

"I've lost my smile and I can't find it anywhere!" he cried.

His friends, the toddlers knew exactly what to do.

They gave the Bibalibet a great, big... HUG!

"How do you feel now?" they asked him.

"I feel all warm and fuzzy again." said the Bibalibet.

"You had your smile with you all along!"

Printed in Great Britain
by Amazon